STARTING
SCIENCE

VOLUME 3

CONTENTS

WHAT'S INSIDE YOU?

Susan Meredith

Designed by Lindy Dark
Illustrated by Kuo Kang Chen, Colin King and Peter Wingham

Consultant: Dr Kevan Thorley

CONTENTS

What does your body do?

Your body is made of masses of different parts. Each part has its own important job to do. All the parts have to work properly together to keep you alive and healthy.

Even when you are doing something quite straightforward, like playing, lots and lots of complicated things are going on inside your body.

Your brain tells all the different parts of you what to do.

You listen to the sounds around you using your ears. Your ears also help you to keep your balance.

Your muscles make you move so you can throw and catch a ball.

Your eyes work hard watching the ball carefully.

Sometimes your muscles start to ache. This tells you it is time for a rest.

Feelers in your body, called nerves, tell you what your body is doing and what is happening to it.

Your mouth shapes sounds into words when you talk.

If you fall and graze your knee, a few drops of blood may spill out but your body soon heals itself.

Your body has a framework of bones which helps it to keep its shape whatever you are doing.

2

If you have been sweating a lot, you may feel thirsty.

If it is hot, you may sweat and go red in the face. This is really your body's way of cooling you down.

You can smell the flowers with your nose.

Your food and drink are travelling through your body. You may need to go to the toilet to get rid of some waste.

You may feel your heart beating in your chest. It is pumping blood round your body to give you energy.

What colour are you inside?

You breathe hard to give your body extra energy.

In this book your insides are shown in all different colours so you can see the different parts clearly.

Babies are exploring and learning all the time.

You are growing very, very gradually all the time.

Most of your insides are really a brownish-red colour a bit like meat.

Eating

Your body needs food and drink to keep working properly.

Using your teeth

You use your teeth to make your food small enough to swallow. Your front teeth are a different shape from your back teeth. Can you feel the difference with your tongue?

Two sets of teeth

Your first set of teeth are called milk teeth because they grow when you are a baby. There are 20 of these.

The milk tooth will eventually fall out as the adult tooth grows up underneath it.

There are 32 teeth in a full adult set. Nobody really knows why people grow two sets of teeth.

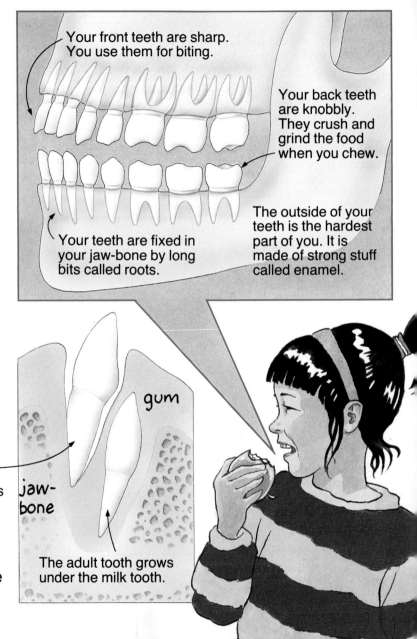

Your front teeth are sharp. You use them for biting.

Your back teeth are knobbly. They crush and grind the food when you chew.

Your teeth are fixed in your jaw-bone by long bits called roots.

The outside of your teeth is the hardest part of you. It is made of strong stuff called enamel.

gum

jaw-bone

The adult tooth grows under the milk tooth.

4

Food

Different foods do different jobs in your body. You need to eat small amounts of lots of different kinds of food to stay really healthy.

Potatoes, rice, pasta, bread and sweet foods give you energy.

Milk, cheese and yoghurt make your bones and teeth strong.

Foods such as meat, fish and eggs make you grow and help to repair your body.

Fruit and vegetables have vitamins in them. These keep your body working efficiently.

Cleaning teeth

It is important to clean your teeth well, especially last thing at night.

Tiny bits of food and drink stick to your teeth even though you cannot feel them.

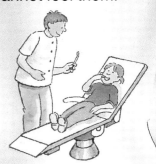

If the bits are left on your teeth, chemicals called acids are made. The acids make holes in your teeth.

Where your food goes

Before your body can use the food you eat, it has to be changed into microscopically tiny bits inside you. It has to be so small it can get into your blood. This is called digestion.

Digesting food

Your food is digested as it goes through a long tube winding from your mouth to your bottom. The tube has different parts, shown here.

Three-day journey

A meal stays in your stomach for about four hours. It takes about three days to travel right through you.

Food starts being digested in your mouth. Your spit has a digestive juice in it which breaks up the food.

The food goes down your gullet into your stomach.

Your stomach is a thick bag. Here the food is churned up and mixed with stomach juice. It becomes like soup.

Your small intestine is all coiled up but is really about as long as a bus. Juices finish digesting your food here.

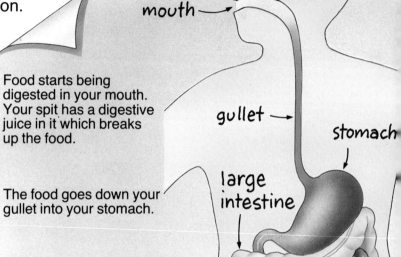

mouth →

gullet →

stomach

large intestine

small intestine

rectum

6

The digested food seeps through the thin walls of your small intestine into your blood.

digested food

intestine wall

blood

Your blood carries the food all round your body.

Water from your food and drink goes into your blood through the walls of your large intestine.

Some bits of food cannot be digested. You push them out of your rectum when you go to the toilet.

Waste water

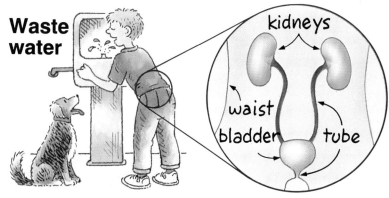

kidneys

waist

bladder   tube

Any water that your body does not need is turned into urine (wee) in your kidneys. These are in your back.

How food moves along

food

Muscles squeeze here.

Food is pushed along.

Food does not slide through you. It is squeezed along by muscles in your digestive tube.

Urine is stored in a bag called a bladder. You can feel your bladder getting full when you need to go to the toilet.

Tummy rumbles

The sound you hear when your tummy rumbles is food and air being squeezed along your digestive tube.

Why do you breathe?

Before your body can use the energy which is in your food, the food has to be mixed with oxygen. Oxygen is a gas which is in the air all around you. When you breathe in, you take oxygen into your body.

How you breathe

The air you breathe is sucked up your nose or into your mouth, down your windpipe and into your lungs.

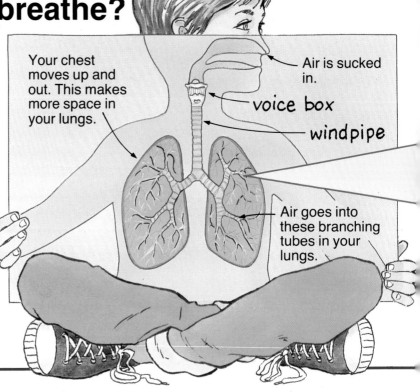

Your chest moves up and out. This makes more space in your lungs.

Air is sucked in.

voice box

windpipe

Air goes into these branching tubes in your lungs.

Voice box

mmm..

The lumpy bit in your neck is your voice box. It is at the top of your windpipe.

Can you feel a sort of wobbling there when you say a loud "mmm" sound?

When you breathe out, air goes through some stretchy cords in your voice box. If there is enough air, the cords wobble like guitar strings when you play them. This makes sounds. Your mouth shapes the sounds into words.

At the ends of the tubes in your lungs are bunches of air sacs. These fill up with air like balloons.

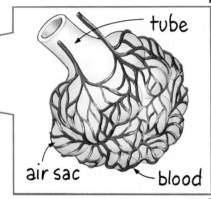

Oxygen seeps through the air sac walls into your blood.

Your blood carries the oxygen round your body. The oxygen mixes with digested food to give you energy.

A waste gas called carbon dioxide is made. Your blood carries this back to your lungs.

When you breathe out, air is squeezed out of your lungs. The air has carbon dioxide in it.

Your chest moves in so there is less space in your lungs.

Air is squeezed out.

Can you feel your chest moving in and out as you breathe?

Hiccups

The sound is the cords in your voice box closing suddenly.

There is a large muscle below your lungs. This moves up and down as you breathe. Sometimes it gets out of control and you get hiccups.

Choking on food

Your windpipe is very close to your gullet.

gullet

When you choke on your food, you say it has "gone down the wrong way". This is true. It has gone down your windpipe instead of your gullet.

9

What is blood for?

The main job of your blood is to carry food and oxygen to all parts of your body. It also collects waste, such as carbon dioxide, so you can get rid of it.

How blood moves

Your blood is flowing round your body all the time in thin tubes called blood vessels. It is kept moving by your heart.

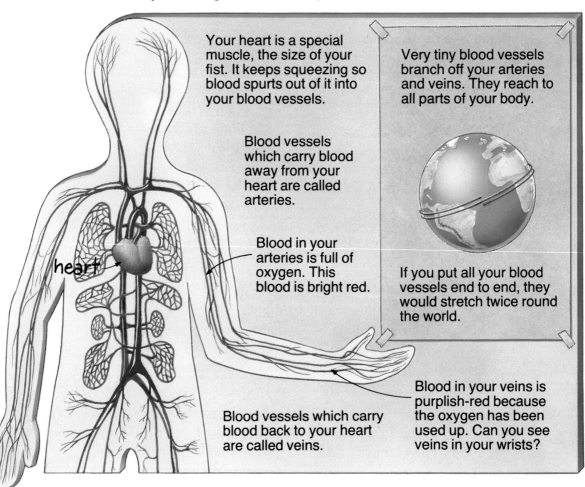

Your heart is a special muscle, the size of your fist. It keeps squeezing so blood spurts out of it into your blood vessels.

Blood vessels which carry blood away from your heart are called arteries.

Blood in your arteries is full of oxygen. This blood is bright red.

heart →

Very tiny blood vessels branch off your arteries and veins. They reach to all parts of your body.

If you put all your blood vessels end to end, they would stretch twice round the world.

Blood vessels which carry blood back to your heart are called veins.

Blood in your veins is purplish-red because the oxygen has been used up. Can you see veins in your wrists?

What is blood?

If you looked at a drop of blood through a microscope, you would see that it had lots of bits floating in it.

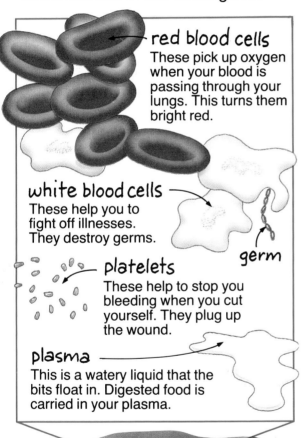

red blood cells
These pick up oxygen when your blood is passing through your lungs. This turns them bright red.

white blood cells
These help you to fight off illnesses. They destroy germs.

germ

platelets
These help to stop you bleeding when you cut yourself. They plug up the wound.

plasma
This is a watery liquid that the bits float in. Digested food is carried in your plasma.

Heartbeats

An adult's heart beats about 70 times a minute; a child's beats 80 to 100 times.

You can hear people's hearts beating. The sound is made by valves. These are like gates in the heart. They slam shut after each spurt of blood has gone through.

Being energetic

Exercise makes your heart and lungs stronger.

When you are being energetic, you need more food and oxygen to keep going. That is why your heart beats faster and harder, and why you breathe faster and deeper.

11

Your skin

Your skin is like a bag which holds your body together. But it has other jobs too. It works all the time to protect you from the outside world.

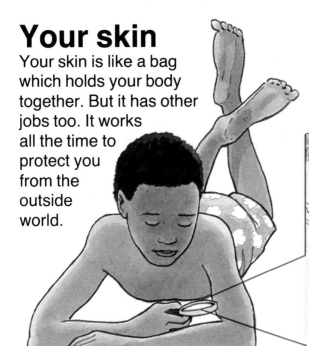

Your skin is only about 2mm thick over most of your body. This picture makes it look much thicker so you can see inside it.

Your hairs grow out of deep pits. Can you see that you have hair on your body as well as on your head?

Blood vessels bring food and oxygen to your skin.

Red in the face

More blood in your skin makes you look red.

When you get hot, the blood vessels in your skin widen. This means that more blood flows near the surface and makes you look red. The air cools down the blood, and you.

Goosepimples

When furry animals get goosepimples, air gets trapped in their fur and helps to keep them warm.

When you are cold, your hair muscles tighten up and make the hair on your body stand on end. This is what makes goosepimples. Goosepimples are not much use to humans.

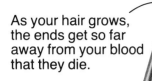

As your hair grows, the ends get so far away from your blood that they die.

The skin you can see is dead because it is too far from your blood vessels.

Sweat is made in sweat glands. It is mainly water and salt. Have you ever tasted the salt?

Your hairs have muscles attached to them.

Your dead skin gets worn away. New skin grows up from below to replace it.

This is a store of fat, which comes from your food. Fat helps to keep you warm and can be used for energy.

Your hair and skin are coated with oil, which is made here. The oil helps stop water soaking into your skin.

You feel things with nerve endings like this one.

Sweat comes out of holes called pores. The air cools you down as it dries the sweat on your skin.

Nails

Fair or dark?

Dark skin is better protected from the sun than fair skin.

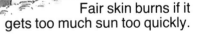

Fair skin burns if it gets too much sun too quickly.

Your nails are a bit like animals' claws. They are made of extremely hard skin.

Some people's skin is darker than others': it has more of a dye called melanin in it.

More melanin is made in strong sunshine. This helps to protect you from the sun.

Messages from outside you

You tell what is happening outside you in five different ways: you see, hear, touch, taste and smell things. This is called using your senses.

How you see

Your eyes have special nerve endings in them which react to light. Light bounces off everything you see.

The light goes into your eyes through the black dot in the middle. The dot is really a hole called the pupil.

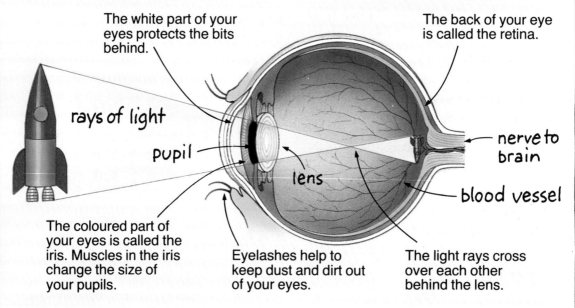

The white part of your eyes protects the bits behind.

The back of your eye is called the retina.

rays of light

pupil

lens

nerve to brain

blood vessel

The coloured part of your eyes is called the iris. Muscles in the iris change the size of your pupils.

Eyelashes help to keep dust and dirt out of your eyes.

The light rays cross over each other behind the lens.

Behind the pupil is a clear disc called a lens. This bends the light in a special way so that an upside-down picture of what you are looking at fits onto the back of your eye.

The nerve endings which react to light are on the back of your eye. They send the picture along a nerve to your brain. Your brain turns the picture back the right way up.

Tears

Tears are made under your top eyelids.

Nobody knows why people cry when they are upset.

Every time you blink, tears wash over your eyes and clean them.

Tears drain into your nose through the inside corners of your eyes.

Big or small pupils

You can watch your pupils changing size. Look at them first in a brightly lit place, then in a dimmer one.

When it is dark, your pupils get bigger to let in as much light as

possible. When it is bright, they shrink to protect your eye.

Wearing glasses

Glasses are lenses. They help the lenses in people's eyes to get the picture onto their retina properly.

Tasting

Your tongue has tiny spots called taste buds on it. These have nerve endings in them which sense different tastes.

Can you see the taste buds if you look at your tongue in a mirror?

Smelling

Nerve endings in your nose tell you about smells. Your senses of smell and taste often work together.

If your nose is blocked up with a cold, you can't taste as much.

Hearing and touching

How you hear

Sounds affect nerve endings right inside your ears.

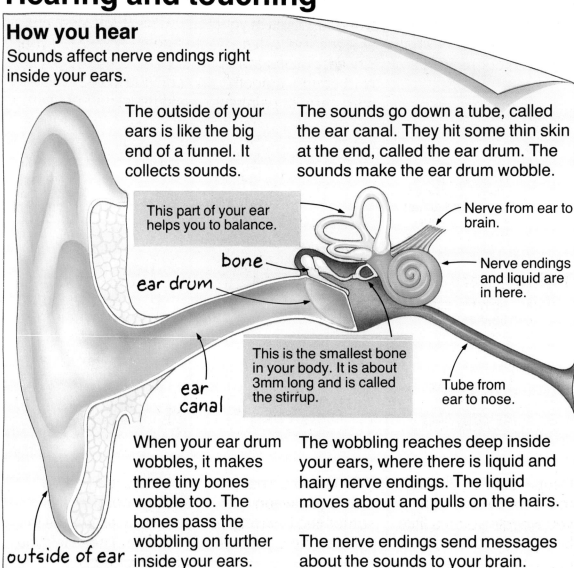

The outside of your ears is like the big end of a funnel. It collects sounds.

The sounds go down a tube, called the ear canal. They hit some thin skin at the end, called the ear drum. The sounds make the ear drum wobble.

This part of your ear helps you to balance.

Nerve from ear to brain.

bone

ear drum

Nerve endings and liquid are in here.

ear canal

This is the smallest bone in your body. It is about 3mm long and is called the stirrup.

Tube from ear to nose.

outside of ear

When your ear drum wobbles, it makes three tiny bones wobble too. The bones pass the wobbling on further inside your ears.

The wobbling reaches deep inside your ears, where there is liquid and hairy nerve endings. The liquid moves about and pulls on the hairs.

The nerve endings send messages about the sounds to your brain.

Balancing

The balance part of your ear tells your brain what position your head is in.

When you know where your head is, you can adjust the rest of your body to balance.

Twitchy ears

Many animals can move their ears to search for sounds.

People cannot usually move their ears. Can you waggle yours a little bit if you concentrate really hard?

Touching and feeling

Nerve endings in your skin tell your brain whether things are hot, cold, rough, smooth, soft, hard, or painful.

You have lots and lots of nerve endings in your fingers, the soles of your feet, and in your lips and tongue.

A tiny hurt in a place with lots of nerve endings can feel enormous.

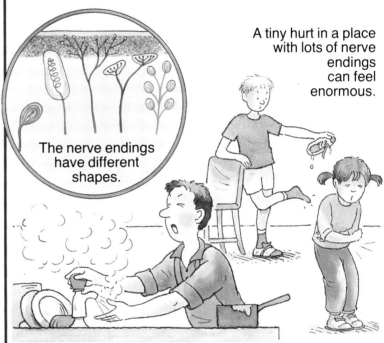

The nerve endings have different shapes.

Pain is useful really. It warns you when something is wrong so you can save yourself from harm.

You have pain nerve endings deep inside your body as well as in your skin. These tell you when you are ill.

Inside your head

Your brain controls the rest of your body and makes sure that all the different parts of you work properly together. Your brain makes sense of what happens to you. It makes you able to think, learn and feel.

Brain and nerves

Your brain is connected to all parts of your body by nerves. These are a bit like telephone wires. Messages go to and from your brain along them.

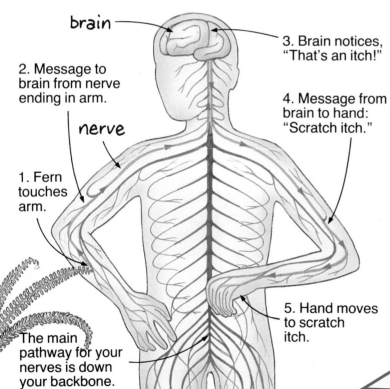

brain

2. Message to brain from nerve ending in arm.

nerve

1. Fern touches arm.

The main pathway for your nerves is down your backbone.

3. Brain notices, "That's an itch!"

4. Message from brain to hand: "Scratch itch."

5. Hand moves to scratch itch.

Body electricity

The messages which go along your nerves are electrical. They are called nervous impulses.

Your funny bone is very close to a nerve. The shooting pain you get when you bang it is a nervous impulse.

Nervous impulses travel at lightning speed. You can't normally feel them.

Learning

Eyes see fruit.

Brain thinks, "I've seen those before. They taste nice."

Message to hand: "Pick up!"

Your brain helps you to learn. It sorts out and stores all the messages it is sent. You work out what new messages mean by remembering old ones.

Sleeping

Dreaming may be a way of making sense of what has happened to you.

Your brain keeps working even when you are asleep. It makes sure your heart keeps beating and that you keep breathing and digesting food.

Parts of the brain

Different parts of your brain deal with different sorts of messages. There are some parts that nobody knows much about. They are probably to do with thinking, remembering and making decisions.

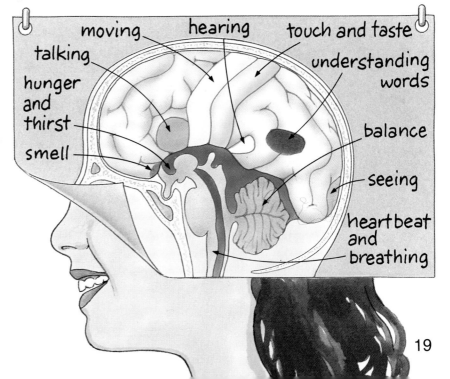

moving

hearing

touch and taste

talking

understanding words

hunger and thirst

smell

balance

seeing

heart beat and breathing

What makes you move?

You are able to move because of the way your muscles, bones, brain and nerves all work together.

Your skeleton

Your skeleton has more than 200 bones. Besides helping you to move, your bones stop your body losing its shape and collapsing. Bones also protect other parts of your body.

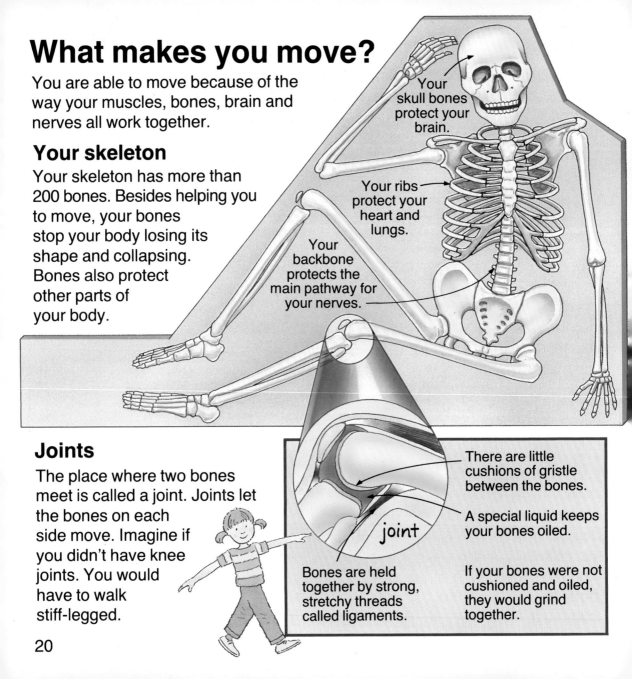

Your skull bones protect your brain.

Your ribs protect your heart and lungs.

Your backbone protects the main pathway for your nerves.

Joints

The place where two bones meet is called a joint. Joints let the bones on each side move. Imagine if you didn't have knee joints. You would have to walk stiff-legged.

joint

There are little cushions of gristle between the bones.

A special liquid keeps your bones oiled.

Bones are held together by strong, stretchy threads called ligaments.

If your bones were not cushioned and oiled, they would grind together.

Muscles

All over your skeleton are stretchy muscles. They are fastened to your bones by strong cords called tendons.

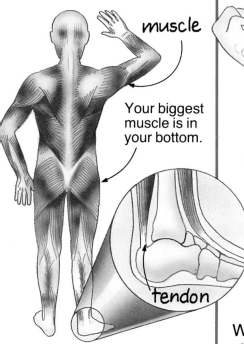

muscle

Your biggest muscle is in your bottom.

tendon

The biggest tendon is in your heel. This looks and feels a bit like a bone but isn't one. You can press it in.

How muscles work

Muscles have nerve endings in them. When you want to move, your brain sends a message to them. This tells the muscle to get shorter. As it does, it pulls on a bone and moves it.

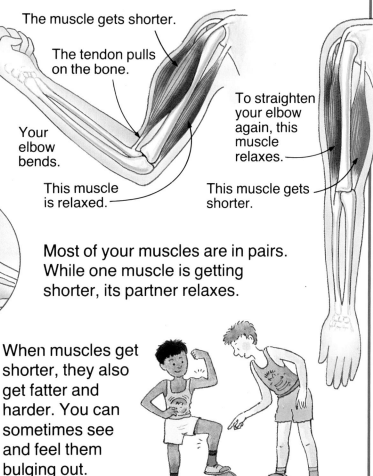

The muscle gets shorter.

The tendon pulls on the bone.

Your elbow bends.

This muscle is relaxed.

To straighten your elbow again, this muscle relaxes.

This muscle gets shorter.

Most of your muscles are in pairs. While one muscle is getting shorter, its partner relaxes.

When muscles get shorter, they also get fatter and harder. You can sometimes see and feel them bulging out.

21

What is your body made of?

All the parts of your body are made of tiny living bits called cells. These are so small that you can only see them with a powerful microscope. You have millions of cells.

Below you can see what a group of skin cells looks like under a microscope.

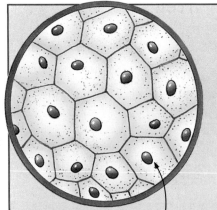

This part controls the way the cell works. It is called the nucleus.

Each of your cells is about two-thirds water. Food and oxygen mix together inside your cells to give you energy.

Chromosomes

The nucleus of each cell has special threads in it called chromosomes. These carry the instructions the cell needs to live, grow and work. Chromosomes are made of a chemical called DNA.

This picture shows part of a chromosome. The instructions for the cell are in code.

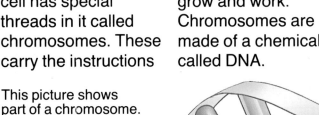

Different kinds of cells

Cells are different shapes and sizes depending on what job they have to do. Here are some examples.

nucleus

Messages travel along your nerves. Nerve cells are very long.

Nerve endings are like feelers.

Muscle cells are long and thin but they can get shorter and fatter. This makes you move.

Cells in your nose and windpipe have tiny hairs on them. These waft germs and dust away from your lungs.

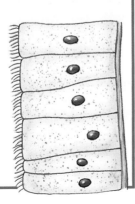

Growing

Until you are about 18, your body keeps making more and more cells. This makes you get bigger.

New cells are made by a cell splitting in two.

a cell

The cell takes in goodness from food and swells up.

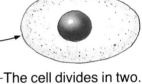

The cell divides in two.

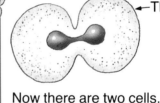

Now there are two cells.

Body repairs

Even when you are grown up, your body has to make some new cells. These replace cells that wear out and die. Some cells live longer than others.

Cells in your intestines get worn away by food and only live for about six days.

Amazing facts and figures

All together you have over 50 billion cells in your body. (A billion is a million million.)

All the nerves in your body, put end to end, would stretch for over 70km (43.5 miles).

Your brain needs so much oxygen that it uses almost one fifth of all the oxygen you breathe in.

You are born with about 350 bones in you body. As you grow up, many of these join together. Adults have just over 200 bones.

Average-sized adults have about 5l (10.5pts) of blood in their body. An average-sized seven year old has about 3l (6pts).

About 50 hairs drop out of your head every day even though you do not notice it. New hairs grow to take their place though.

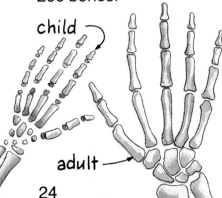

24

WHERE DID DINOSAURS GO?

Mike Unwin

Designed by Ian McNee

**Illustrated by Andrew Robinson,
Toni Goffe and Guy Smith**

Edited by Cheryl Evans

**Consultant: Dr Angela Milner
(The Natural History Museum, London)**

CONTENTS

What were dinosaurs?

Dinosaurs were animals that lived millions of years ago, before there were any people. Today there are no dinosaurs left.

Dinosaur means 'terrible lizard'. People called them this because their skeletons looked like giant lizards' skeletons.

Now scientists know dinosaurs were not lizards. This part of the book explains what they really were.

Giants

Most dinosaurs were much bigger than the lizards you can see today.

Diplodocus was one of the longest dinosaurs. It grew up to 27m (89ft) long. That's as long as a tennis court.

The Komodo Dragon is the longest lizard alive today. It grows up to 3m (10ft) long.

No more dinosaurs

65 million years ago dinosaurs became extinct. This means they disappeared forever. Nobody is sure why this happened. But experts have many ideas about it, as you will discover in this book.

A long time ago

The time before people began to write is called prehistory. It is split into three different parts called eras. This picture tells you a bit about each one.

225 million years ago.

↓

Palaeozoic Era

Trilobites were small creatures that lived in the sea during the Palaeozoic Era. This was before dinosaurs.

Dinosaurs appeared here.

↑

This arrow has colours to show the different eras.

Mesozoic Era

Dinosaurs lived during the Mesozoic Era. This era can be split up into three different periods. Here you can see a dinosaur from each period.

Dinosaurs disappeared here.

↓

Dinosaurs were prehistoric animals that lived on Earth for 154 million years. People have only been around for about the last three million years.

Plateosaurus lived during the Triassic Period.

Allosaurus lived during the Jurassic Period.

Styracosaurus lived during the Cretaceous Period.

65 million years ago.

↑

Caenozoic Era

Brontotherium was a big animal that lived during the Caenozoic Era. This was after dinosaurs.

People appeared about three million years ago.

People have not been here for long compared to dinosaurs.

This book will tell you lots of things about dinosaurs. It will also help you to understand what might have happened to them.

What's left of dinosaurs

Experts have learned about dinosaurs by studying fossils. Fossils are the remains of animals that died a long time ago and have been turned into stone. They are all that is left of the dinosaurs now.

How fossils were made

When a dinosaur died, its soft parts soon rotted away. But its hard skeleton was left.

If the dinosaur was in a muddy place such as the bottom of a lake, the skeleton sank into the mud.

As more mud covered the skeleton, the bottom layers were squashed and hardened into rock.

Over time, special minerals in the rock turned the skeleton to stone. This made it into a fossil.

Dinosaur jigsaw puzzle

Scientists who study fossils are called palaeontologists. They try to fit all the fossil pieces of a dinosaur together to find out what it looked like and work out how it lived.

This rock is 150 million years old.

A special hammer is used to chip rock from around the bones.

Palaeontologists photograph each fossil before they remove it, so they know exactly where it was found.

Fossils are found in places that were once covered by water. Here you can see a dinosaur fossil being dug out of a cliff.

Getting it wrong

Sometimes palaeontologists make mistakes. When scientists first put *Iguanodon* together, they found one bone that did not seem to fit the rest of the skeleton. They decided that it belonged on *Iguanodon's* nose, like a rhinoceros's horn. But when they found more fossils they realized that this bone was a spike on *Iguanodon's* thumb.

At first they thought *Iguanodon* looked something like this.

This is the bone that muddled scientists.

Now they know *Iguanodon* looked more like this.

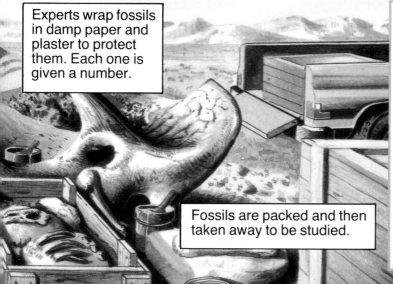

Experts wrap fossils in damp paper and plaster to protect them. Each one is given a number.

Fossils are packed and then taken away to be studied.

More to come

In 1965, palaeontologists in Mongolia found the huge arms of a dinosaur they called *Deinocheirus*. They are still looking for its body.

Deinocheirus's arms were longer than a man.

Dinosaur origins

It helps to understand why dinosaurs disappeared if you know where they came from. Most scientists think all living things gradually change. This change is called evolution.

Your environment is the area where you live. Evolution makes animals change, or evolve, to suit their environment.

Giraffes live in an environment with tall trees. They have evolved long necks to reach the leaves at the top.

From water to land

Here you can see how dinosaurs evolved over millions of years.

Over 350 million years ago, no animals lived on the land. But where pools began to dry up, some fish began to leave the water.

Eusthenopteron was a fish that used its strong fins like legs.

How to survive

Sometimes environments can change. Animals that are suited to the changes survive, but others die. A famous scientist, Charles Darwin, called this natural selection.

Not everybody believes in evolution and natural selection. Many people believe God created Earth and put animals on it as they are now.

350 million years ago, animals with legs, called amphibians, evolved. They lived on land, but they had to be close to water to lay eggs.

Dimetrodon was a reptile. Its legs stuck out from the sides of its body.

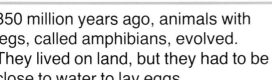

Ichthyostega was an amphibian. Its legs carried it low over the ground.

310 million years ago, animals called reptiles evolved. Their bodies were now suited to life on the land. They had dry, scaly skin to protect them from the sun.

230 million years ago, some reptiles evolved stronger and straighter legs. These were the first dinosaurs.

Natural selection at work

Peppered Moths show how a changing environment can make animals evolve.

1. Some Peppered Moths are dark and some are pale. 200 years ago there were more pale moths.

2. Pale moths were the same colour as trees, so birds caught more dark ones, which were easier to see.

3. When factories were built, smoke made the trees darker. Birds now found it easier to catch pale moths.

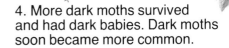

4. More dark moths survived and had dark babies. Dark moths soon became more common.

31

Shapes and sizes

Dinosaurs evolved into many different sizes. Some were quite small. Others were much bigger than any land animals alive today.

Brachiosaurus was one of the biggest dinosaurs. It could weigh more than 50 tonnes (51 tons). That's the same as nine elephants.

Brachiosaurus was as high as a three storey house.

Its back bones were light but very strong to help carry its heavy body.

Strong legs supported its weight.

Keeping warm

Animals cannot survive if they get too hot or too cold. A dinosaur's temperature changed with the heat of the Sun. In cool weather, dinosaurs got cold.

The biggest dinosaurs were so huge that it took them a very long time to cool down. So their great size helped them to keep warm.

Using a sail

Spinosaurus had a special sail on its back to keep its body at the right temperature. As the Sun moved, *Spinosaurus* changed position.

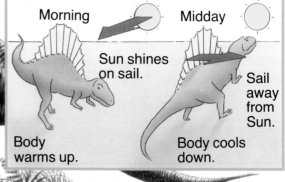

Morning

Sun shines on sail.

Body warms up.

Midday

Sail away from Sun.

Body cools down.

Different shapes

Dinosaurs evolved into different shapes for different reasons.

Ceratopians had huge heads with bony frills and sharp horns. *Triceratops* was the biggest ceratopian. It was 11m (36ft) long and weighed 5.4 tonnes (6 tons).

Parasaurolophus called to others by making loud trumpeting noises through its crest.

Parasaurolophus had a bony beak for tearing off plants to eat, and a bony crest on its head.

Triceratops had sharp horns to keep enemies away.

A bony frill protected its neck and held strong muscles for working its jaws.

Euoplocephalus was a heavy dinosaur covered in armour and spikes for protection.

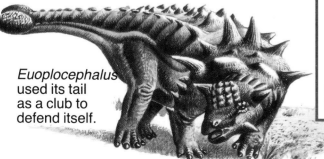

Euoplocephalus used its tail as a club to defend itself.

Make a dinosaur

You could make a *Euoplocephalus* with balls of playdough, used matches and drawing pins.

Roll a big ball for the body.

Roll smaller balls for the head, legs and club.

Roll a sausage shape for the tail.

Use broken matches for the spikes.

Use drawing pins for the armour.

Dinosaur life

Fossil clues help experts to find out how dinosaurs lived. This also helps them to discover what changes may have made dinosaurs die out.

Clues about food

Some dinosaurs had sharp teeth and strong claws. This shows that they ate meat. *Tyrannosaurus rex* was one of the biggest meat-eaters ever. It was as heavy as an elephant and as long as a bus.

Tyrannosaurus rex had sharp teeth for cutting meat.

Strong claws for tearing open its prey.

How you eat

People can eat many different kinds of food. You have different teeth for different jobs. Look at your mouth in a mirror and feel inside with clean fingers.

Can you feel sharp front teeth for cutting and knobbly back teeth for grinding?

Other dinosaurs had special teeth for eating plants. *Corythosaurus* was a plant-eater. It chewed on tough leaves and twigs.

Corythosaurus's jawbone shows hundreds of small teeth for grinding plants.

Corythosaurus →

Fossil dinosaur droppings can show what dinosaurs ate.

Pine needles in dropping.

34

Eggs

Scientists know that some dinosaurs laid eggs, because they have found lots of fossil ones. The biggest eggs are over 30cm (1ft) across.

Baby *Protoceratops* hatched from eggs laid in the sand to keep them warm.

Staying together

Lots of fossil *Triceratops* have been found together. This shows that they probably lived in herds.

Experts think adult *Triceratops* surrounded their babies to protect them from danger.

Fossil footprints

Velociraptor was a fierce hunter. It was only two metres (6.5 ft) long, but its fossil footprints are spaced far apart. This shows how fast *Velociraptor* could run.

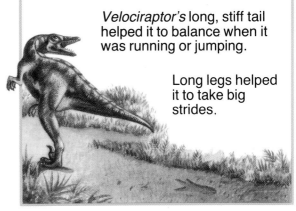

Velociraptor's long, stiff tail helped it to balance when it was running or jumping.

Long legs helped it to take big strides.

Fighting

Some dinosaurs that lived in herds fought each other to decide upon a leader. The thick skull bone of the male *Pachycephalosaurus* was probably used to protect it in fights.

Pachycephalosaurus fought with their heads, like goats do.

35

Alongside dinosaurs

While dinosaurs were living on the land, other prehistoric reptiles were living in the sea and the air. Interestingly, they disappeared at exactly the same time as dinosaurs.

Sea monsters

Huge reptiles lived in the sea. Their long, smooth bodies made them good swimmers. Their legs evolved into flippers to help them swim.

Ichthyosaurs grew up to 12m (38ft) long. They did not lay eggs, but gave birth to their young underwater.

Large flippers pulled plesiosaurs through the water.

Long necks helped them to catch fish.

Plesiosaurs grew up to 12m (38ft) long. They came onto land to lay their eggs.

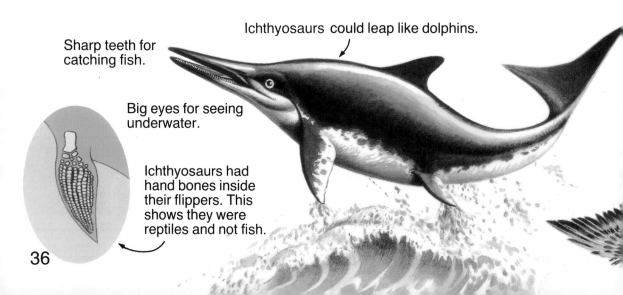

Ichthyosaurs could leap like dolphins.

Sharp teeth for catching fish.

Big eyes for seeing underwater.

Ichthyosaurs had hand bones inside their flippers. This shows they were reptiles and not fish.

In the air

Pterosaurs were flying reptiles. They had wings made of skin, just like bats today. They also had very light bones to help them fly. Some were no bigger than a sparrow. Others were the size of a small aircraft.

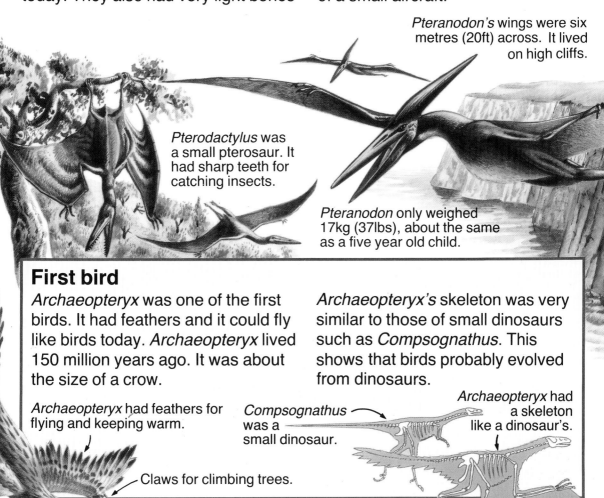

Pteranodon's wings were six metres (20ft) across. It lived on high cliffs.

Pterodactylus was a small pterosaur. It had sharp teeth for catching insects.

Pteranodon only weighed 17kg (37lbs), about the same as a five year old child.

First bird

Archaeopteryx was one of the first birds. It had feathers and it could fly like birds today. *Archaeopteryx* lived 150 million years ago. It was about the size of a crow.

Archaeopteryx's skeleton was very similar to those of small dinosaurs such as *Compsognathus*. This shows that birds probably evolved from dinosaurs.

Archaeopteryx had feathers for flying and keeping warm.

Compsognathus was a small dinosaur.

Archaeopteryx had a skeleton like a dinosaur's.

Claws for climbing trees.

Why did they die?

Experts know when dinosaurs died out but they are still not sure why. There are different ideas about what might have happened. Now scientists know many of these ideas are wrong.

Finding out from rocks

Fossil dinosaurs are found in rocks from the Mesozoic Era. But there are none in rocks that are newer than this.

No dinosaur fossils

Newer rock lies on top of Mesozoic rock.

Dinosaur fossils

Mesozoic rock is over 65 million years old.

This shows that dinosaurs all became extinct 65 million years ago, at the end of the Mesozoic Era.

Too big?

Some scientists thought dinosaurs grew so huge that they could not support their own weight.

Now experts know that big dinosaurs had very strong skeletons.

Small dinosaurs became extinct too. So size can not explain why they all died out.

Dying of diseases?

Some scientists thought diseases made dinosaurs extinct.

Some dinosaurs did have diseases, but they evolved to survive these. Now experts know that disease on its own can never make a type of animal extinct.

Beaten by mammals?

During the Mesozoic Era, a new kind of creature called mammals evolved. (You can read more about them later.)

Some experts thought mammals ate all the dinosaurs' food.

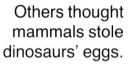

Others thought mammals stole dinosaurs' eggs.

Now scientists are sure that mammals did not make dinosaurs extinct. Mammals only became important after dinosaurs died out.

Poisonous flowers?

The first flowering plants evolved during the Cretaceous Period. Some experts thought they had chemicals that poisoned dinosaurs.

Now scientists know that new kinds of dinosaurs evolved especially to eat the new plants.

End of the line

During the Mesozoic Era, new dinosaurs always evolved to take the place of others. But at the end of the Era, dinosaurs all died out together, and no more evolved to replace them.

Something must have happened that killed all the dinosaurs and stopped new ones from evolving. The next four pages tell you more about this.

DEAD END

Big changes

The environment changed in many different ways while dinosaurs lived on Earth. Scientists think this might explain why dinosaurs died out.

Changes in plants

Many different kinds of plants evolved during the Mesozoic Era.

These plants lived during the Triassic and Jurassic Periods.

Horsetails

Cycads

These plants lived during the Cretaceous Period.

Flowering plants

Hardwood trees

Changes in plants meant dinosaurs' food was always changing too. But these changes were so gradual that dinosaurs could evolve to keep up.

Changes in the weather

The climate is the kind of weather that any place usually has.

Earth had a warm climate for most of the Mesozoic Era.

But at the end of the Cretaceous Period it became cooler. Experts think that cold weather helped to make dinosaurs extinct.

Dinosaurs had no fur or feathers to help store their body heat. Most of them were too big to warm up again after a long, cold winter.

Changes in the Earth's surface

The Earth's surface is broken into large pieces called plates. These move around so that continents are always slowly changing positon. This is called continental drift.

As the plates move, the Earth's environment and climate change. Some experts think this made dinosaurs extinct. These maps show how the Earth has changed.

During the Triassic Period, there was just one big continent called Pangaea. The climate was warm all around the world.

During the Cretaceous Period, Pangaea split up into new continents and oceans were left in between them. Earth's climate became cooler.

This is what the Earth looks like today. The continents are still moving, but it happens too slowly for you to tell.

In the sea

As the land changed, so did the sea. Some experts think this killed millions of tiny sea creatures called Foraminifera, and other animals that ate them.

Foraminifera and many other sea creatures died out with dinosaurs.

Too slow

Continental drift takes a very long time. On its own, it does not explain why dinosaurs and other creatures all died out so suddenly.

A sudden change

Now scientists think dinosaurs died out because something violent suddenly changed the Earth's climate. Here is what may have happened.

What broke the food web?

Many scientists think a big lump of rock from outer space, called an asteroid, struck the Earth at the end of the Mesozoic Era.

The asteroid was probably 10 to 15 km (6 to 9 miles) across.

Nothing left to eat

All living things in any environment depend upon each other for their food. This is called a food web.

Caterpillars eat leaves

Shrews eat caterpillars

Owls eat shrews

If the dinosaurs' food web broke at the end of the Mesozoic Era, they would have died out. Here you can see why.

No plants

Plant eaters died

Meat eaters died

Where it landed

There are clues that an asteroid hit what is now Yucatan in Mexico.

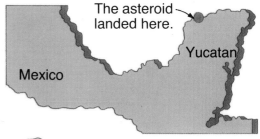

The asteroid landed here.

Yucatan

Mexico

Experts have found tiny glass beads like this around the area. They are made of rock that melted when the asteroid struck the earth.

No sunlight

All living things close to where the asteroid struck were killed. Dust and gases filled the air all round the world. Sunlight was blocked out and the world became cold and dark.

Without sunlight, all the plants died.

When plants died, the food web broke down. This killed dinosaurs, and they soon became extinct.

How plants grow

You can see how plants need sunlight. Put some damp paper towel on a saucer and scatter cress seeds on it.

Leave the saucer in sunlight so the seeds can grow.

Cover some shoots with an egg cup.

Take the egg cup off after a week. The shoots without any sunlight will have died.

Volcanoes

65 million years ago there were also some huge volcanic eruptions in what is now India. These might have caused as much damage as an asteroid.

Some experts think dust and gases from these volcanoes might have blocked out the sunlight too.

Too hot?

When the asteroid struck, it threw up water vapour as well as dust. After the dust settled, water vapour stayed in the air. It trapped the heat of the sun, so the Earth heated up like a giant greenhouse.

Just as dinosaurs would have been killed by cold, they also would have died if it was too hot.

After dinosaurs

Not everything became extinct at the end of the Mesozoic Era. Plants grew up from seeds that had survived, and soon other animals began to fill the places left by dinosaurs.

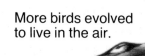
More birds evolved to live in the air.

Small mammals lived in the trees and forests.

Some reptiles, such as crocodiles and turtles, still lived in fresh water.

About mammals

Mammals are animals that can keep their bodies warm all the time. Most mammals have fur or hair and do not lay eggs. They give birth to babies and feed them on milk.

Purgatorius lived 70 million years ago when dinosaurs were still around. It probably slept during the day, and came out at night. All later mammals evolved from animals like this.

Staying alive

Mammals' warm bodies helped them to survive when the climate changed and dinosaurs died out. They were also small enough to burrow holes and escape from the cold or heat.

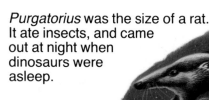
Purgatorius was the size of a rat. It ate insects, and came out at night when dinosaurs were asleep.

Different kinds of mammal

The time since dinosaurs died out is called the Caenozoic Era. Many different mammals have evolved and died out during this time. Here you can see some that are now extinct.

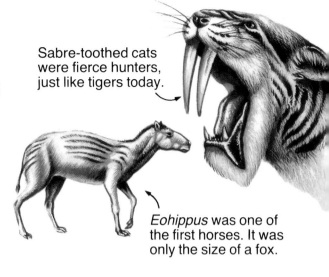

Sabre-toothed cats were fierce hunters, just like tigers today.

Paraceratherium was the largest ever land mammal. It was 8m (26ft) tall. That's six times as high as a man.

Eohippus was one of the first horses. It was only the size of a fox.

Dinosaur relatives

Tuataras lived over 150 million years ago, at the same time as dinosaurs. Some still live in New Zealand today.

Tuatara

Chaffinch

Modern birds evolved from prehistoric birds like *Archaeopteryx,* and they still have very similar skeletons to dinosaurs. This shows that birds are dinosaurs' closest relatives today.

Out of the trees

People are mammals. Most experts think we evolved from creatures like apes that lived in the trees about 10 million years ago.

The first people were hunters who could walk upright on two legs. They learned how to use tools, build shelters and make fire.

Today

Since dinosaurs died out, many other living things have become extinct. Today most extinctions are caused by the things people do.

Damage to wildlife

Wildlife means all the wild plants and animals living in the world. The main danger to wildlife comes from people damaging or changing the environment where it lives.

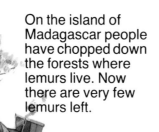

On the island of Madagascar people have chopped down the forests where lemurs live. Now there are very few lemurs left.

Pollution is waste left by people, such as rubbish or poisonous chemicals. Pollution in the environment harms everything that lives there.

Oil spilled in the sea kills many sea birds, such as cormorants.

Hunting

If animals are hunted too much, they can become extinct. People hunt animals for many different reasons.

Ocelots and other wild cats are hunted just for their beautiful skins. Now they are becoming very rare.

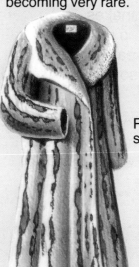

People make ocelot skins into fur coats.

Dodos were once hunted for food. They became extinct 300 years ago.

Living together

It is important to look after the environment and protect wildlife. All living things are connected to each other by food webs. If one thing disappears, many others may suffer.

For example, snakes eat rats. In parts of Africa, people killed lots of snakes. Soon there were too many rats. They began to eat people's crops, so people suffered.

Safe places

There are many ways to help wildflife. People can stop hunting animals and protect the places where they live.

Over 15 thousand elephants live in Hwange wildlife park in Africa. Here they are safe from hunters.

How to help

There are lots of things you can do to help protect your environment. Here are some ideas.

Always put your rubbish in a bin.

Never damage plants or pick wild flowers.

Try not to waste things. Re-use plastic bags and take glass bottles to a bottle bank if you can.

You could join a conservation group near your home. They organize lots of activities. You can find out about them at your nearest library.

Keep watch

Today you can only see dinosaurs in museums. But you can still see many other fascinating creatures living on Earth. It is up to everyone to stop them from disappearing as dinosaurs did.

Where to see dinosaurs

Dinosaur fossils have been discovered all over the world. In most countries you can visit places to see dinosaurs and find out more about them.

Stuck in the rock

At the Dinosaur National Monument in Utah, U.S.A., there is a cliff full of dinosaur bones. Here you can see the remains of giants such as *Diplodocus*, *Apatasaurus* and *Stegosaurus.*

Biggest bones

The world's largest dinosaur skeleton is a *Brachiosaurus* from East Africa, which you can see at the Berlin Natural History Museum in Germany.

A recent find

In London's Natural History Museum you can see lots of dinosaurs and other fossils. They include the fish-eating dinosaur *Baryonyx*, which was discovered in England in 1986.

Giant steps

At Peace River Canyon in Canada, you can see lots of fossil footprints. These show where dinosaurs walked across the river bed millions of years ago.

Eggs from the desert

Hundreds of fossil *Protoceratops* eggs have been found in the Gobi desert in Mongolia. You can see them at the Academy of Sciences in Ulan Bator.

There is probably a place near you where you can see dinosaurs and other fossils. You can find out about museums at your local library.

WHERE DOES RUBBISH GO?

Sophy Tahta

Designed by Lindy Dark
Illustrated by Colin King and Guy Smith
Edited by Cheryl Evans
With thanks to Friends of the Earth

CONTENTS

Consultant checker: Chris Murphy

All sorts of rubbish

You probably throw things away when they are old or broken or when you just don't want them anymore.

But your rubbish is only a tiny part of the mountains of waste thrown out each year all over the world.

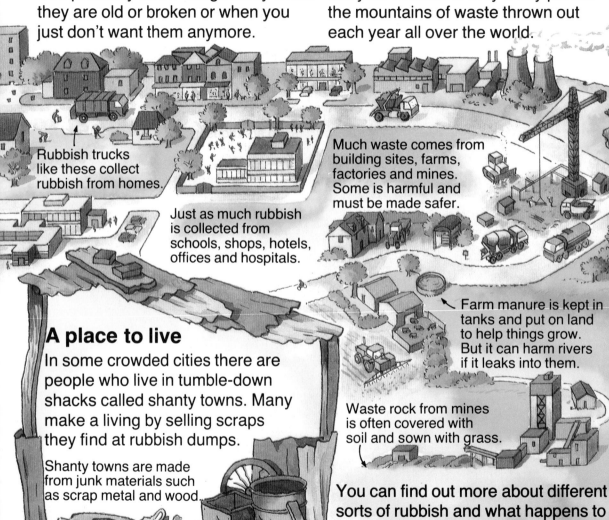

Rubbish trucks like these collect rubbish from homes.

Just as much rubbish is collected from schools, shops, hotels, offices and hospitals.

Much waste comes from building sites, farms, factories and mines. Some is harmful and must be made safer.

Farm manure is kept in tanks and put on land to help things grow. But it can harm rivers if it leaks into them.

A place to live

In some crowded cities there are people who live in tumble-down shacks called shanty towns. Many make a living by selling scraps they find at rubbish dumps.

Waste rock from mines is often covered with soil and sown with grass.

Shanty towns are made from junk materials such as scrap metal and wood.

You can find out more about different sorts of rubbish and what happens to them in this part of the book.

50

Space junk

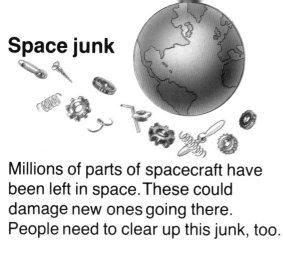

Millions of parts of spacecraft have been left in space. These could damage new ones going there. People need to clear up this junk, too.

Rubbish in the wrong place

Litter is rubbish that is dropped on the ground, into rivers or in the sea.

Ships throw tons of old nets and plastic rubbish in the sea each day, even though this is not allowed.

Sea litter can trap and choke turtles, seabirds, whales, fish and seals.

Broken glass and sharp cans left on the ground can cut animals.

Clues to the past

People called archaeologists study the things which others once threw away or left behind, to find out more about how they used to live.

Some of the things archaeologists dig up are thousands of years old.

You can help to stop litter from hurting animals or spoiling the view by putting yours in bins.

Not everything you throw away is rubbish. Notice the sorts of things you throw away each week. Most can be used again, as you will see.

51

Clearing up

Rubbish from shops, homes, schools, and so on is put into all sorts of bins or bags. These are collected and emptied into rubbish trucks which crush the rubbish to pack more in.

Bins on wheels

Places such as schools or shops put rubbish in big, plastic or metal bins with wheels. Some homes do too.

Lots of trucks are fitted with special lifts. These lift up and tip out bins of all sizes.

Rubbish trucks carry rubbish from hundreds of bins and bags.

This truck is filled up and emptied several times a day.

This is called a packer blade. It slides down, scoops rubbish into the truck and squeezes it against a panel.

Bin lids keep smells and rubbish in and animals out.

This powerful machinery could be dangerous if you get too near.

As more rubbish is crammed in, this panel slides back to make more room.

Rubbish must be collected often or it can start to rot and attract rats and flies which spread diseases.

52

Cleaning the street

All sorts of machines are used to clean roads. In some places a street cleaner also sweeps pavements and empties litter bins into a cart.

This hose can be pulled out to suck up dead leaves and litter.

This pipe sucks rubbish into the truck through a wide nozzle.

Nozzle

Strong brushes wash and scrub the road.

Water is sprayed out of holes in the nozzle and brushes.

People who collect rubbish and clean streets start early when roads are clear. Some even work at night.

Special collection

Venice in Italy has canals for streets. Rubbish is collected there by barges.

In cities such as Paris in France, special scooters suck dog mess into a box with a hose.

Everest is the highest mountain in the world.

So much litter has been left on Mount Everest, that a team of climbers has been to pick it up.

On the move

In many towns, rubbish trucks dump their rubbish at a place called a transfer station. From here it goes to big holes in the ground called landfills.

Tipped out

At some transfer stations, rubbish is tipped straight into a machine called a compactor.

This back end lifts up.

Rubbish trucks are too slow and heavy to go far. They will only go straight to a landfill if there is one near enough.

This panel slides forward, pushing rubbish out.

The rubbish falls down a chute called a hopper.

Box

Boxed in

A huge metal bar at one end of the compactor shoves rubbish into a long metal box clamped to the other end.

Rubbish from four trucks is pressed or compacted into one box. This saves space.

Compacter ram

This bar is called a ram. It slides to and fro under the hopper.

Full boxes slide away from the compactor on metal rails, so that this door can be shut.

54

Taken away

An overhead crane lifts the boxes onto long, flat trucks.

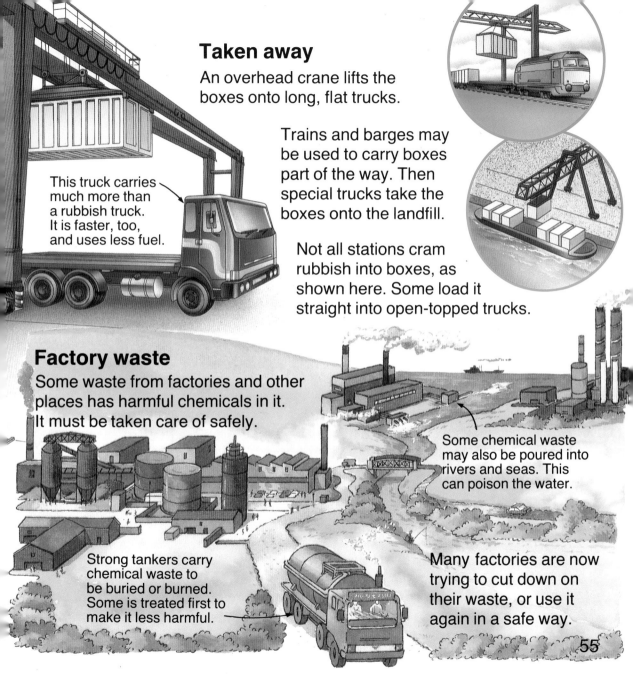

This truck carries much more than a rubbish truck. It is faster, too, and uses less fuel.

Trains and barges may be used to carry boxes part of the way. Then special trucks take the boxes onto the landfill.

Not all stations cram rubbish into boxes, as shown here. Some load it straight into open-topped trucks.

Factory waste

Some waste from factories and other places has harmful chemicals in it. It must be taken care of safely.

Some chemical waste may also be poured into rivers and seas. This can poison the water.

Strong tankers carry chemical waste to be buried or burned. Some is treated first to make it less harmful.

Many factories are now trying to cut down on their waste, or use it again in a safe way.

Rotting away

Each day tons of rubbish are tipped out at landfills, crushed into layers and buried. Some of it rots away.

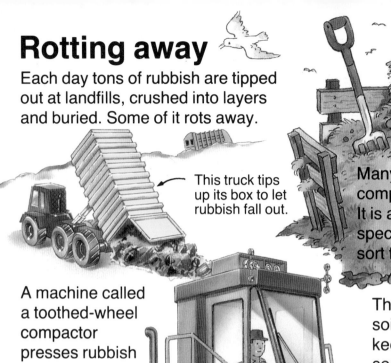

This truck tips up its box to let rubbish fall out.

A machine called a toothed-wheel compactor presses rubbish into layers.

These heavy wheels and spikes help to flatten the rubbish.

Rotting food

Vegetable and garden waste rots into a rich muck called compost.

Many people make their own compost to help things grow. It is also made at a few special waste centres which sort food waste with machines.

The rubbish is covered with soil at the end of each day to keep litter and smells in and seagulls, rats and flies out.

This shovel scoops up and spreads the rubbish.

Some landfills are made in old quarries which are no longer used.

56

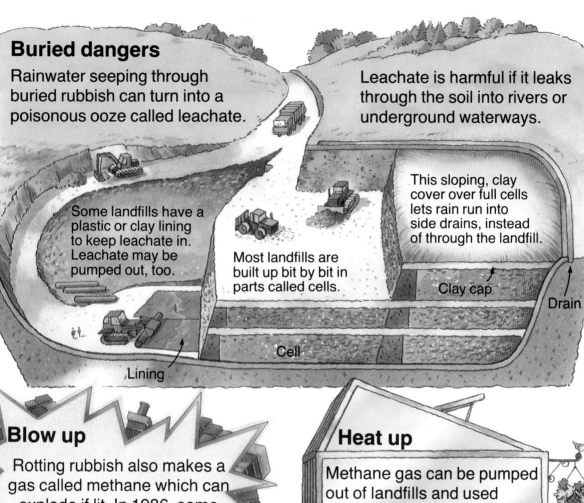

Buried dangers

Rainwater seeping through buried rubbish can turn into a poisonous ooze called leachate.

Leachate is harmful if it leaks through the soil into rivers or underground waterways.

This sloping, clay cover over full cells lets rain run into side drains, instead of through the landfill.

Some landfills have a plastic or clay lining to keep leachate in. Leachate may be pumped out, too.

Most landfills are built up bit by bit in parts called cells.

Clay cap

Drain

Cell

Lining

Blow up

Rotting rubbish also makes a gas called methane which can explode if lit. In 1986, some leaked into a house in Britain. It was lit by a spark and blew up. Luckily, no-one was killed.

Heat up

Methane gas can be pumped out of landfills and used safely to make electricity, or to heat homes, brick ovens and even greenhouses.

57

Up in flames

In big cities, rubbish may be burned in a place called an incinerator. This saves space in landfills, but gives off harmful gases, too.

1 Down the pit

Rubbish trucks tip rubbish straight into a deep pit at the incinerator.

3 Burning up

The furnace must be terribly hot to make sure the rubbish burns properly and gives off fewer harmful gases.

A person in a control room works the crane.

2 Into the furnace

A crane grabs rubbish out of the pit and drops it down a chute into a giant oven called a furnace.

This grab crane moves along beams and lifts up and down.

Hot air, gas and smoke go this way.

Furnace

Air is blown over and under the rubbish to make it burn well.

Ash goes this way.

This sloping floor is called a grate. Moving rollers on top carry the burning rubbish along.

These rollers turn and break up the rubbish to make it burn better.

58

4 Hot air

Heat from incinerators can be used to make electricity or to heat homes. In the city of Yokohama in Japan, it is used to heat swimming pools.

6 Dirty smoke

There are laws to make sure harmful smoke and gases are made cleaner, but some may still escape from the chimney.

Gases may be cleaned in tanks like this, with a chemical called lime.

Tanks like this collect dust and soot on big, metal plates or long tubes of cloth.

Chimney

5 Cool ashes

The ash is cooled in water and put on a moving belt. A magnet may be used to pick out some metal things which did not burn.

Magnet

Water

Ashes go to landfills.

Metal is crunched into blocks, sold for scrap and used again.

Out at sea

Some chemical waste used to be burned at sea in ships. Most countries have now stopped this as the waste gases were not always cleaned properly.

59

Down the drain

Each time you take a bath or flush the toilet, the waste water runs down the drainpipe to underground pipes called sewers. These take it to a place called a sewage works.

Sewage works are very important because they help to keep rivers clean and healthy.

This bend is always full of water to stop smells from coming back up.

Drainpipes

Rainwater often runs down drains into sewers.

Inside pipes take waste to drainpipes outside.

Waste in sewers is called sewage.

Sewers from homes join bigger ones under the street. These join giant sewers which go to the sewage works.

Sewers run downhill if possible. Sewage is pumped along uphill pipes.

By the sea

In some seaside towns, sewage pours out of a long sewer pipe into the sea. It may be cleaned a little first, but often it is not.

This raw sewage can make the sea horrid to swim in.

In the country

In some homes in the country, sewage goes to underground tanks. Every year or so it is pumped out by a tanker and taken to a sewage works.

This is called a septic tank.

These pipes let some liquid drain slowly into the soil.

At the sewage works

Sewage flows through many tanks at the sewage works. These take out different things to make it cleaner.

1 This screen traps wood, rags and other large things.

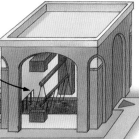

2 Grit sinks to the bottom of this tank and is pumped out.

3 The sludgy part sinks down in this tank. From here sewage water and sludge go to different tanks.

4 Sewage water goes here where it is mixed with a special liquid.

This liquid has lots of tiny, living things called bacteria in it.

These feed on dirt on the water to help to clean it.

Sewage water   Sewage sludge

6 Sewage sludge goes here where bacteria in the sludge turn some of the dirt into methane gas. This gas can be used to run the works.

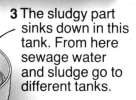

7 The thickest sludge sinks down here, leaving water on top.

It is spread on land, burned or dumped at sea. Some countries have now stopped dumping it at sea.

5 The special liquid is pumped out of this tank and used again. The water goes into rivers.

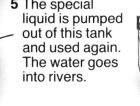

61

Dangerous waste

Waste which poisons water, soil or air is called pollution. There are laws to stop people from causing pollution, or to make them pay to have it cleaned.

In the rivers

Waste from sewage works and farms can pollute rivers with chemicals called phosphates and nitrates.

Phosphates come from sewage and cleaning liquids and powders.

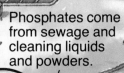

Nitrates are added to land to help things grow. Some wash into rivers.

These chemicals help to make too many plants called algae grow.

Algae use up air and light needed by other plants and animals.

In the sea

Oil tankers can pollute seas if they leak, or if they break the law and wash out their tanks at sea.

Oil clogs up birds' wings and chokes fish.

Oil spills are expensive and difficult to clean.

This nuclear power station uses nuclear power to make electricity.

Below ground

Some waste from nuclear power stations can be dangerous for thousands of years. It must be looked after very carefully.

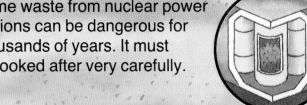

Some nuclear waste is set in concrete and sealed in drums and boxes. These will one day be stored deep underground.

Acid rain

Waste gases from cars, factories and power stations pollute the air and some can turn rain sour, or acid. More gases could be cleaned before leaving chimneys.

Acid rain poisons trees and lakes.

It also wears away statues and buildings.

Greenhouse gases

Some waste gases trap heat in the air like the glass of a greenhouse. This could warm up the Earth, causing parts of it to dry up. People need to stop making so many of these gases.

Heat escaping into space.

Heat from the sun.

Heat trapped by greenhouse gases.

Greenhouse gases build up in the air above Earth.

Car fumes

Car fumes make a poisonous, chemical smog when the sun shines on them. They also send out lead, which is harmful to breathe.

A filter called a catalytic converter can be fitted in car exhausts to clean gases which make smog and acid rain.

Drivers can use petrol without any lead in it.

The ozone layer

The ozone layer is a layer of gas around Earth which protects living things from harmful sunrays. Gases called CFCs break down this layer.

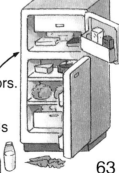

Some CFCs are used in refrigerators. Most countries have agreed to stop using all CFCs by the year 2000.

Using things again

Using rubbish again is called recycling. This saves using up so many things from the ground, called raw materials, to make new things. Some of these raw materials will one day run out.

Here are some things you can save which can be recycled, or used again.

Clothes, toys, books, old stamps and coins, can go to charity shops, which can sell them again.

Lots of this rubbish has been used to wrap or pack things. Using less packaging would make less rubbish.

No waste

In Cairo, the capital city of Egypt, rubbish is collected by a group of people called the Zabaleens.

This rubbish will be sorted and sold to people who can use it again.

Food and garden waste can be turned into compost.

Paper, bottles, cans and rags can be made into new things. Plastic can also be recycled in this way.

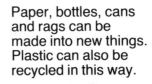
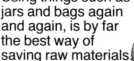

Using things such as jars and bags again and again, is by far the best way of saving raw materials.

Paper chain

Saved waste paper and cardboard goes to a paper merchant's yard. Here it is sorted, pressed into bales and sent to a paper mill for recycling.

At the mill the paper is soaked in tanks of hot water and whisked into a mush called stock.

A machine spreads the stock onto a moving wire mesh to make paper.

As the stock drains, tiny thread-like fibres join up to make a big, sheet of paper.

Pumps underneath suck water out.

Heavy rollers squeeze water out of the paper.

The paper is fed onto a band of felt, which moves around different rollers.

Hot rollers dry it.

Polished rollers smooth it.

This roller winds it into a reel.

Make your own paper

Try recycling your own paper. It will help to show you what happens to paper at a paper mill.

Soak torn bits of newspaper overnight in a little water. Mash it with a fork.

Drain it. Roll it with a rolling pin and let it dry.

Trim the edges and paint it. You could use your paper as a table mat.

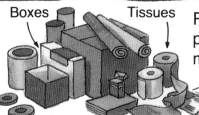

Boxes   Tissues

Recycled cardboard and paper go to factories to make some of these things.

← Newspapers

More things to save

Recycling also saves energy. Energy comes from burning fuels such as oil. It takes much less energy to recycle things such as cans and bottles than it takes to make new ones from scratch.

Sorting cans

Cans are made from different metals which can be melted down and used again. Use a magnet to see which metal yours are made from.

Hold the magnet to the side.

Most cans are made from steel which sticks.

Steel cans are picked out at some transfer stations with giant magnets.

Many drinks cans are made from aluminium which does not stick.

Recycling aluminium cans saves almost all the energy it takes to make new ones.

Less pollution

Recycling also cuts down on pollution from incinerators, landfills and mines, as less rubbish is burned or buried and fewer raw materials are dug up. This makes the countryside look nicer, too.

Saving bottles

Any old jars and bottles you save for recycling can be melted down with these other things at a glass factory, to make new ones

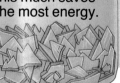

Limestone

Soda-ash

Sand

Old glass can make up to half the amount. Using this much saves the most energy.

66

Sorting rubbish

Rubbish can be collected for recycling in different ways. In many places, you can take your old newspapers, bottles and cans to special bins in the street, called banks.

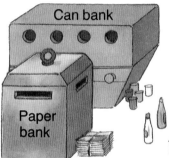

Can bank

Paper bank

Bottle banks

A few banks take plastic bottles, too.

Money back

In some places people pay a bit more for bottled goods in shops. They get this money back when they return the empty bottles.

Some countries also have machines which give a coin for each aluminium can put in.

Sorting at home

In some places, people sort their rubbish into different bins or bags at home, to be collected separately.

In parts of Germany food scraps are put into one bin and collected separately to make compost.

Sorting centres

In a few countries, jumbled-up rubbish may be taken to a special waste centre to be shredded and pressed into pellets.

These pellets are burned in factories as a fuel.

Big things

Sometimes people need to get rid of things which are too big to go in the bin. They may be able to have them collected on special days, or they may take them to a recycling centre.

These centres have huge, metal crates for people to put things in. Many have recycling banks, too.

This crate is for garden waste.

Battery bank

Worn clothes and rags can be made into new things such as blankets.

Rag bank

This tank collects old car oil to clean and use again. Pouring oil down drains or on the ground is not allowed, as it can seep into rivers.

Batteries have harmful acids in them which can leak. They can be recycled, but not many places do this yet.

Metal things may be put in a separate crate and sold to a metal merchant for recycling.

Oil bank

Fly-tips

Dumping rubbish in places where it should not be is called fly-tipping. This spoils the towns and countryside.

Full crates are collected by trucks. Anything that cannot be recycled goes to a landfill.

Some rubble from building sites gets fly-tipped, even though this is not allowed.

On the scrap heap

Many old cars end up in a scrapyard. Here they are taken apart and crushed by powerful machines.

Trains and planes

Scrap steel from old bridges, ships, trains and planes is also melted down to make more things.

Useful things, such as engines, may be taken out and sold as spare parts.

This crane lifts the cars into a machine which flattens them.

The squashed cars go to a big scrap yard to be shredded into tiny bits of steel. These bits are melted down at a steel works.

Old batteries

The plastic cases and lead metal plates from car batteries can be recycled, too.

Used tyres

Tyres are difficult to bury or burn. People are always trying to find more ways to recycle them.

69

In the past

For thousands of years most people lived in small, farming villages. They did not have as much as many people have now and they wasted very little.

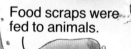

Rotten fence posts were used for firewood.

Food scraps were fed to animals.

Food waste, ash, animal manure and sewage may also have been used to make compost.

Broken tools and clothes were mended.

Toilets in the past

Some castles had tiny rooms in the walls with a hole for a toilet. The waste fell down a chute into the moat or a pit.

These rooms are called garderobes.

About 500 years ago many people in towns used chamber pots, and tipped them out into the street below.

The first flush toilet was made in Britain in 1589 by Sir John Harington, but it was ages before most people had one.

Some rich people had really grand flush toilets.

Rubbish in the cities

About 200 years ago many cities got crowded and dirty as lots of people went to work in the new factories which were being built. Some people earned a tiny bit of money by getting rid of rubbish.

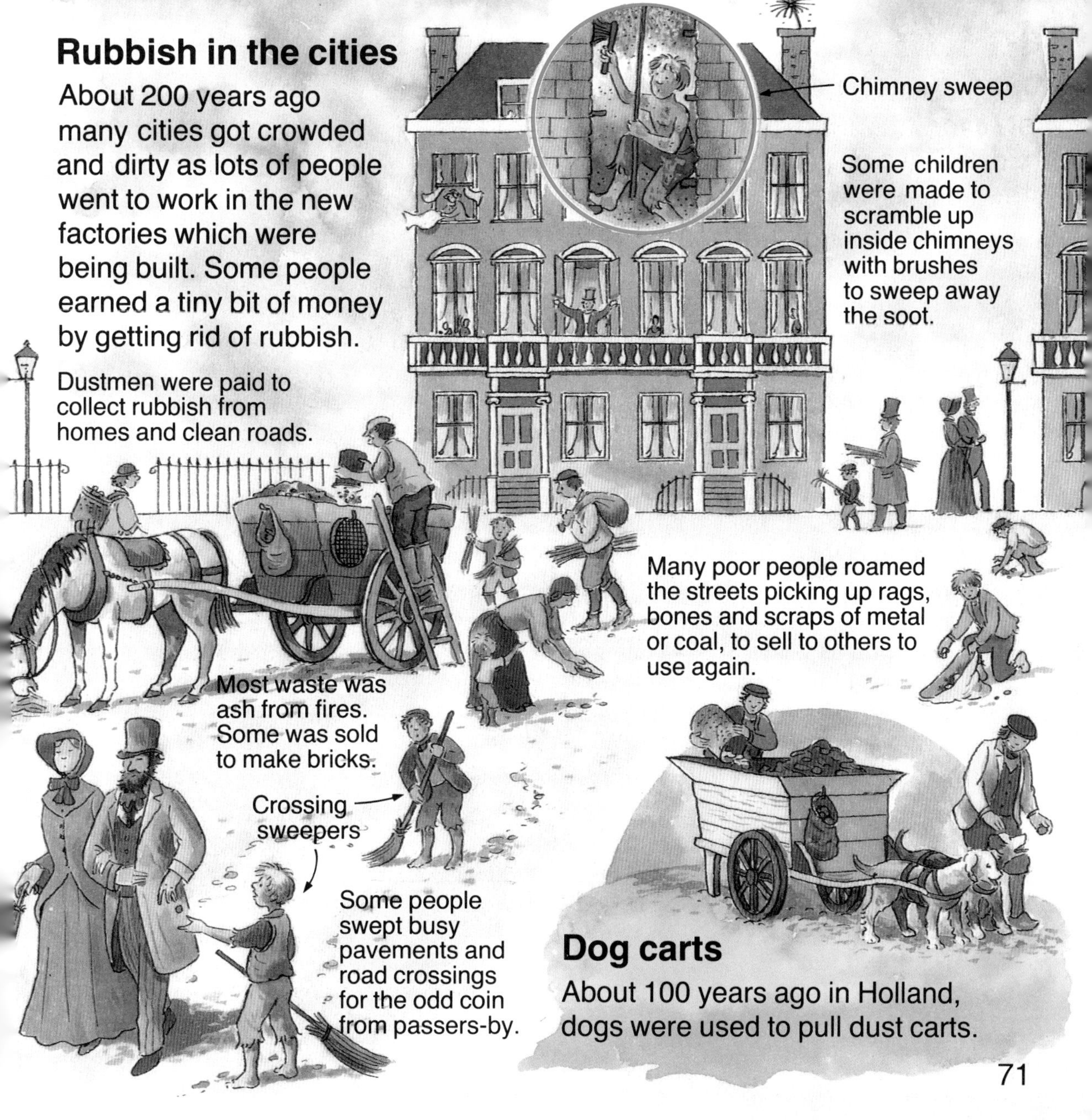

Dustmen were paid to collect rubbish from homes and clean roads.

Chimney sweep

Some children were made to scramble up inside chimneys with brushes to sweep away the soot.

Most waste was ash from fires. Some was sold to make bricks.

Crossing sweepers

Many poor people roamed the streets picking up rags, bones and scraps of metal or coal, to sell to others to use again.

Some people swept busy pavements and road crossings for the odd coin from passers-by.

Dog carts

About 100 years ago in Holland, dogs were used to pull dust carts.

What makes what? quiz

You've seen what can be made from recycled paper in this part of the book.

Now see if you can guess what things are made from these sorts of rubbish.

Empty cans and scrap metal.

Broken jars and bottles.

Old plastic bags, bottles and other plastic things.

Cotton waste from mills.

Unwanted clothes.

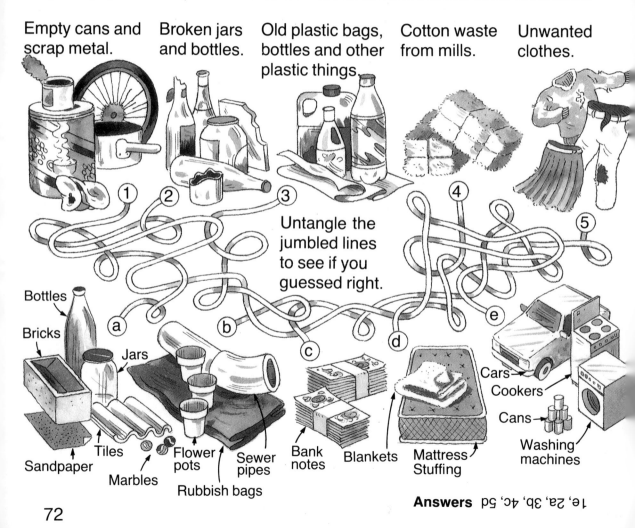

Untangle the jumbled lines to see if you guessed right.

Bottles

Bricks

Jars

Sandpaper

Tiles

Marbles

Flower pots

Rubbish bags

Sewer pipes

Bank notes

Blankets

Mattress Stuffing

Cars

Cookers

Cans

Washing machines

Answers 1e, 2a, 3b, 4c, 5d

WHERE DO BABIES COME FROM?

Susan Meredith

Designed by Lindy Dark

Illustrated by Sue Stitt and Kuo Kang Chen

Consultants: Dr Kevan Thorley
and Cynthia Beverton of Relate, Marriage Guidance Council

CONTENTS

All about babies

As the baby grows, its mother's tummy gets bigger.

Everybody who has ever lived was once a baby and grew in their mother's tummy. This book tells the story of how babies come into the world and begin to grow up.

A baby grows in a sort of hollow bag called the womb or uterus. This is a warm, safe place for it to be until it is big and strong enough to survive in the outside world.

Food and oxygen

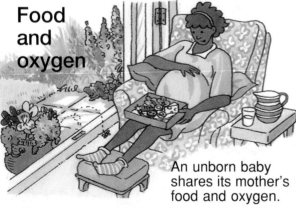

An unborn baby shares its mother's food and oxygen.

The baby needs food to stay alive and grow. It also needs oxygen from the air. But babies cannot eat or breathe in the womb. They get food and oxygen from their mother's blood.

Being born

The baby stays inside its mother for about nine months. That is about 38 weeks. Then it is ready to be born. It gets out of its mother's tummy through an opening between her legs.

74

Feeding

At first the only food a baby needs is milk, either from her mother's breasts or from feeding bottles. She needs to be fed every few hours.

Crying

It is not always easy to figure out what a baby's crying means.

A newborn baby can do nothing for herself, so she requires a lot of attention. Crying is her only way of telling people she needs something.

Baby animals

A cow's tummy gets fatter as her calf grows inside her.

Kittens feed on milk from their mother's nipples.

Many animals grow in their mothers' tummies and are born in the same way as people. They also get milk from their mothers.

Growing up

Babies gradually learn to do more and more for themselves.

Many animals separate from their parents when they are very young. It is years before children can manage without their parents' help.

Starting to grow

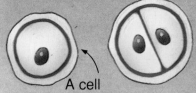

Everybody is made of millions of tiny living bits called cells. A baby starts to grow from just two very special cells, one from its mother and one from its father. Together, these two cells make one new cell.

Dividing cells

A cell

The new cell divides in half to make two cells exactly the same. These two cells then divide to make four cells. The cells continue dividing until a whole ball of cells is made.

Each cell is really no bigger than a period at the end of a sentence.

In the womb

Ball of cells

Womb lining

Womb

The ball of cells settles down in the mother's womb, the place where babies grow. It sinks into the womb's soft cushiony lining and continues to grow.

A month later, the developing baby is still no bigger than a bean, but the dividing cells have started forming the different parts of the baby's body.

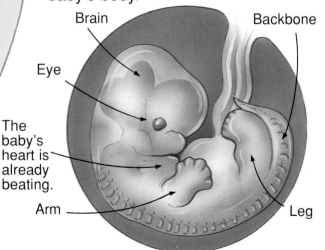

Brain

Backbone

Eye

The baby's heart is already beating.

Arm

Leg

The baby's lifeline

The baby is attached to the lining of the womb by a special cord. The food and oxygen the baby needs go from its mother's blood down the cord and into the baby's body.

Like everybody else, the baby needs to get rid of waste. This goes down the cord from the baby's blood into its mother's blood. Her body gets rid of it when she goes to the toilet.

Blood vessels

This is called the placenta. It grows on the lining of the womb.

The cord is called the umbilical cord.

The placenta is where food, oxygen and waste pass between the mother's blood and the baby's.

The baby floats in a bag of special water. This acts as a cushion and protects the baby from harm.

The baby cannot drown in the water because it does not need to breathe until it is born.

Getting bigger

The baby continues to grow. It moves and kicks, and also sleeps. It can hear its mother's heart beating and noises from outside her body too. Some babies even get hiccups.

Eventually, most babies settle into an upside-down position in the womb.

Some babies suck their thumbs.

77

What is it like being pregnant?

When a mother has a baby growing inside her, it is called being pregnant. While she is pregnant, her body changes in all sorts of ways.

Check-ups

The mother has regular check-ups to make sure she and the baby are healthy. These are given by a midwife or doctor. A midwife is someone who looks after pregnant mothers.

The mother is weighed. She should put on weight as the baby grows.

The mother's blood and urine are tested. This tells the doctor if the mother and baby are well.

Looking after herself

The mother has to take special care of herself. If she is well, the baby is more likely to be healthy too.

It is not good for the baby if the mother smokes, drinks alcohol or takes certain medicines.

She is feeding her baby as well as herself, so she has to eat healthy food.

The mother's body has to work harder than usual, giving the baby what it needs. She has to rest more.

Gentle exercise pumps more blood through to the baby and makes the mother feel better too.

When the mother's tummy gets big, she should not carry heavy things. She may strain her back.

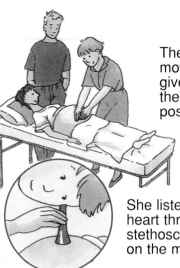

The doctor feels the mother's tummy. This gives her an idea of the baby's size and position.

She listens to the baby's heart through a special stethoscope. She puts it on the mother's tummy.

Photos of the baby

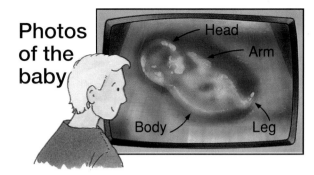

Head
Arm
Body
Leg

A machine called an ultrasound scanner takes moving pictures of the baby in the womb. These appear on a television screen and show everyone how the baby is developing.

Kicking

After about five months, the mother feels the baby moving. Later, it will kick.

You may feel the kicks if you put your hand on the mother's tummy.

Eventually the mother can see her tummy moving and even guess whether a bump is a hand or a foot.

Getting bigger

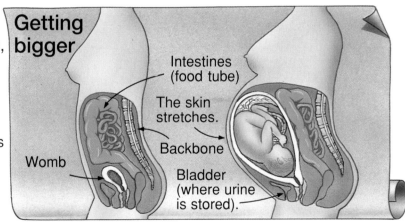

Intestines (food tube)
The skin stretches.
Backbone
Womb
Bladder (where urine is stored).

The mother's womb is normally the size of a small pear. As the baby grows, the womb stretches and other

things in her body get squashed up. This can be a bit uncomfortable but everything goes back to normal later.

Mothers and fathers

The special cells from the mother and father which make a baby start to grow are the sex cells. They are different from each other.

Egg cells

The mother's sex cell is called an egg cell or ovum. She has lots of egg cells stored in her body, near her womb.

Tube

Womb lining

Egg

Ovary

Womb

Tube

Ovary

Vagina

The egg cells are stored in the mother's two ovaries.

Once a month, an egg cell travels from one of the ovaries down one of the tubes leading to the womb.

Every month the lining of the womb gets thick and soft with blood. It is getting ready for a baby to start growing there.

There is a stretchy tube leading from the womb to the outside of the mother's body. It is called the vagina.

Babies are born through the opening of the vagina, which is between the mother's legs.

The vaginal opening is quite separate from the ones for going to the toilet. It is between the two, just behind the one for urine.

This picture shows where the mother's baby-making parts are located.

80

Sperm

The father's sex cell is called a sperm cell. Sperm are made in the father's two testicles. The testicles are in the bag of skin which hangs behind his penis

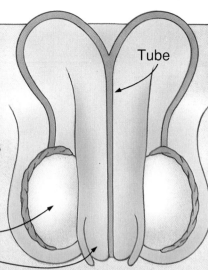

Tube

Testicle

Penis

The father's baby-making parts are between his legs.

Sperm can travel from the testicles along two tubes and out of the end of the penis.

Urine never comes out of the penis at the same time as sperm.

Growing up

Young girls and boys cannot become mothers and fathers. Your baby-making parts do not start working properly until the time when your body starts to look like a grown-up's.

What if a baby doesn't start?

If a baby does not start to grow, the womb's thick lining is not needed. The lining and the egg cell break up and trickle out of the mother's vagina with some blood.

This takes a few days each month and is called having a period. To soak up what comes out, the mother puts things called tampons in her vagina or places pads in her panties.

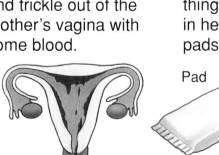

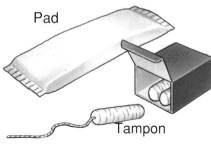

Pad

Tampon

81

How does a baby start?

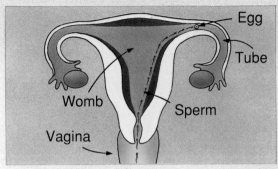

A baby starts to grow when an egg and sperm meet and join together. They do this inside the mother's body. The way the sperm get to the egg is through the mother's vagina.

Sperm cells come out of the opening at the end of the penis and swim up into the mother's womb and tubes. If the sperm meet an egg in the tubes, one of them may join with it.

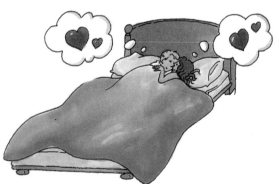

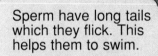

Sperm have long tails which they flick. This helps them to swim.

The mother and father cuddle each other very close. The father's penis gets stiffer and fits comfortably inside the mother's vagina. This is called making love or having sex.

The moment when the egg and sperm join together is called conception or fertilization. Now a baby can start to grow.

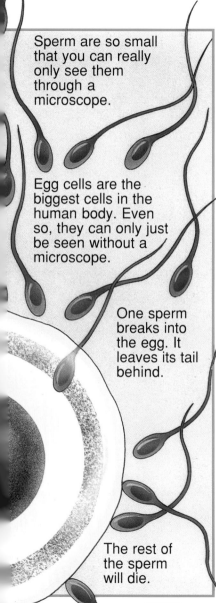

Sperm are so small that you can really only see them through a microscope.

Egg cells are the biggest cells in the human body. Even so, they can only just be seen without a microscope.

One sperm breaks into the egg. It leaves its tail behind.

The rest of the sperm will die.

Pregnant or not?

It is several months before the mother's tummy starts to get

Calendar

If she is pregnant, her monthly periods stop. The lining of the womb is needed for the growing baby.

The hormones may make the mother dislike foods she usually likes or they may make her crave some foods.

bigger but she has other ways of knowing she is pregnant.

Some pregnant mothers feel sick. This is caused by chemicals called hormones in their blood.

Her breasts get bigger and may feel a bit sore. They are getting ready to make milk when the baby is born.

To be sure she is pregnant, the mother's urine is tested to see if it has one of the pregnancy hormones in it.

83

How is a baby born?

After nine months inside its mother, the baby is ready to be born. It has to leave the warm, safe womb and move down the vagina to the outside world. This is called labor, which means hard work.

Labor

The womb is really a very strong muscle. During labor, it keeps on squeezing and squeezing until the baby comes out of it. Each squeeze is called a contraction.

The baby will not need its placenta for much longer.

The mother's other leg has been left out of this picture so you can see the baby clearly.

Vagina

The vagina stretches easily to let the baby pass through. Afterwards it goes back to its normal size.

The contractions pull the womb open and squeeze the baby through the opening.

Placenta

During labor, the bag of water around the baby bursts. The water drains away out of the mother's vagina.

Towards the end of labor, the mother pushes hard to help the baby out. Soon after the baby is born, the placenta and empty water bag come out of the vagina too.

When does labor start?

When the baby is ready to be born, special hormones are made in its blood. These go down the umbilical cord to the mother's body and make the contractions start.

The mother feels the contractions as pains in her tummy.

Most mothers go to hospital to have their baby. Some choose to have theirs at home.

Helping the mother

Having a baby is exciting but can be exhausting and take many hours. A doctor looks after the mother during labor. The father can help too.

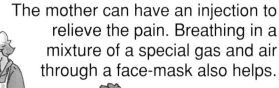

The father might rub the mother's back if it aches, or encourage her to relax and breathe properly.

The mother can have an injection to relieve the pain. Breathing in a mixture of a special gas and air through a face-mask also helps.

The baby's heartbeat

The doctor listens to the baby's heartbeat during labor to make sure it is all right. In hospitals, the heartbeat is sometimes measured by a machine called a monitor.

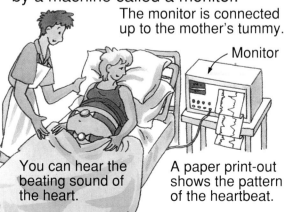

The monitor is connected up to the mother's tummy.

Monitor

You can hear the beating sound of the heart.

A paper print-out shows the pattern of the heartbeat.

What is a Caesarian birth?

Sometimes the baby cannot be born in the usual way. Instead it is lifted out through a cut in the mother's tummy. This is called a Caesarian.

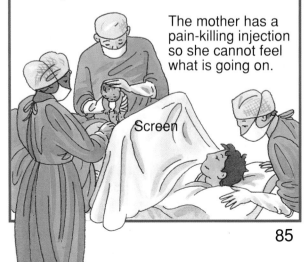

The mother has a pain-killing injection so she cannot feel what is going on.

Screen

Newborn babies

The first thing everyone does as soon as a baby is born is to look between its legs. Is it a girl or a boy?

The doctor checks that there is no liquid in the baby's nose or mouth. Now he can start to breathe.

The cord is cut here. The baby cannot feel it.

A clip stops any bleeding.

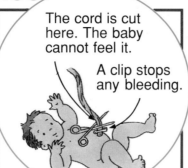

Now that the baby can eat and breathe on his own, he no longer needs his umbilical cord. It is cut off.

Clip

The tiny bit of cord that is left dries up and falls off in a few days. Your tummy button is where your cord was.

The doctor checks that the baby is well and weighs him. He will be weighed often to make sure he is growing.

In the hospital, a newborn baby has a name label put on his wrist. This avoids any mix-up about whose baby he is.

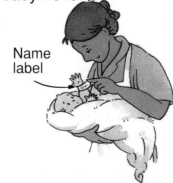

Name label

Getting used to the world

The baby has been safe and comfortable in the womb for nine months. It is probably quite a shock to find herself in the outside world. She may also be tired from the birth.

The baby will get used to her new surroundings better if she is held and spoken to very gently. It may also help if things are kept fairly quiet and dimly lit at first.

The mother starts feeding the baby.

The parents cuddle the baby and start getting to know her. Sisters and brothers come to meet her.

Newborn babies have to be wrapped up warm. Their bodies lose heat quickly.

Some newborn babies are almost bald. Others have a lot of hair. Some have hair on their body too. This soon rubs off.

Babies have a soft spot on their head. Bones gradually grow over it but until then it has to be protected.

Babies born in hospital usually sleep in a see-through cot by their mother's bed.

At first, babies all have blue eyes. The color may gradually change.

Incubators

If a baby is very small or unwell when she is born, she may have to go in an incubator for a while. This is a see-through cot which is all enclosed and very warm.

The parents can touch the baby through windows in the incubator.

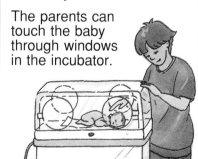

What makes a baby like it is?

The mother's egg and the father's sperm cell together have all the instructions needed for a baby to grow in the way it does.

Chromosomes

The instructions are carried on special threads in the cells. The threads are called chromosomes. The proper word for the instructions is genes.

This picture shows part of a chromosome.

The instructions are in a complicated code a bit like a computer program.

When the egg and sperm join together at conception, the new cell gets the chromosomes from both of them. Copies of these are passed to every cell in the baby's body.

The baby's cells have 46 chromosomes each, 23 from the egg and 23 from the sperm.

Because you have chromosomes from both your parents, you will take after both of them. The mixture of the two sets of instructions also means that you are unique.

Some things about you, like the way you look, depend a lot on your chromosomes. Other things depend as well on the type of life you have after you are born.

You are more likely to become a good swimmer if you are taken to the swimming pool a lot.

Girl or boy?

Whether a baby is to be a girl or a boy is settled at conception. It depends on one chromosome in the egg and one in the sperm. These are the sex chromosomes.

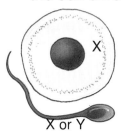

X or Y

The sex chromosome in all egg cells is called X. Half the sperm also have an X sex chromosome but half have one called Y.

If a sperm with an X chromosome joins with the egg, the baby is a girl.

Girls have two X sex chromosomes.

XX

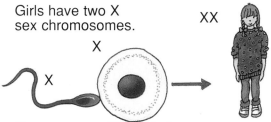

X

X

If a sperm with a Y chromosome joins with the egg, the baby is a boy.

Boys have one X and one Y sex chromosome.

XY

X

Y

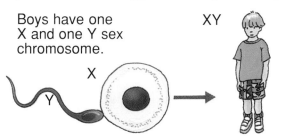

Twins

Twins grow in their mother's womb together and are born at the same time, one by one. A few twins are identical, which means exactly alike. Most twins are non-identical, which means not exactly alike.

Sometimes, when the new cell made at conception splits in two, each half grows into a separate baby. These twins are identical because they come from the same egg and sperm.

Identical twins are always the same sex.

Sometimes, two separate sperm meet and join with two different eggs at the same time, and two babies grow. These twins are not identical because they come from different eggs and sperm.

Non-identical twins may be the same sex or one of each sex.

89

What do babies need?

Babies need to have everything done for them. They have to be fed and kept warm, comfortable and clean.

They need lots of love and attention, and they need interesting things going on around them.

Breast-feeding

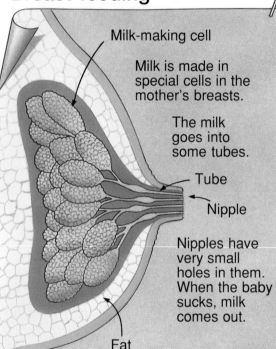

Milk-making cell

Milk is made in special cells in the mother's breasts.

The milk goes into some tubes.

Tube

Nipple

Nipples have very small holes in them. When the baby sucks, milk comes out.

Fat

When a mother has a baby, milk starts being made in her breasts. Hormones in her blood make this happen. Whenever the baby sucks at the breast, more milk is made.

If a mother is breast-feeding, she needs to eat well, drink plenty and get extra rest.

Breast milk is made from substances in the mother's blood and is the best food for a baby. It has chemicals called antibodies in it. These help the baby to fight off illnesses.

Bottle-feeding

If babies are not being breast-fed, they have special powdered milk instead. This is usually made from cow's milk but is then altered to make it more like breast milk.

Special powdered milk is mixed with water for a baby's bottle.

Ordinary cow's milk is too strong for babies.

Cuddles

A young baby's neck is not strong enough to hold her head up. Her head needs something to rest on all the time.

A cushion will keep your arm from aching.

Babies need a lot of cuddles to make them feel safe and contented. They need to be handled gently though.

Diapers

A young baby may need as many as eight diaper-changes in a day.

If a wet or dirty diaper is not changed, the baby is more likely to get a diaper rash.

Babies do not know in advance that they need to go to the toilet. They only learn to tell as they get older.

Babies cannot fight off germs like older people, so their bottles have to be especially clean. This is done by sterilizing, which means getting rid of germs.

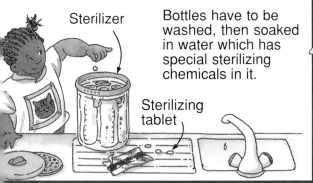

Sterilizer

Bottles have to be washed, then soaked in water which has special sterilizing chemicals in it.

Sterilizing tablet

Sleeping

Babies have no idea of day and night at first.

It can take them a long time to learn to sleep through the night.

Some young babies sleep for as many as 18 hours a day. They wake up every few hours to eat though, even in the night. Nobody knows why some babies sleep more than others.

A new baby in the family

This is an exciting, enjoyable time but it is also hard work. And it can take a while to get used to having a brand-new person in the family.

A new baby takes up so much of her parents' time and attention that older brothers and sisters can even feel a bit jealous at first.

The mother's body

It takes a few weeks for the mother's body to go back to normal after having the baby, and she needs to rest. Both parents will be tired from getting up in the night to the baby.

Helping

You could gather things that are needed for the baby and put them away.

It is useful for the parents to have help around the house at first. As the baby gets older, you could help by, for example, giving her a bottle.

Crying

A baby's crying is hard to ignore. This is useful for the baby: it makes people look after him. Babies cry for various reasons. Nobody really knows why some cry more than others.

Is the baby hungry? Is he uncomfortable or in pain? Is he too hot or too cold, bored, tired, lonely or frightened?

Babies cannot wait for things. They have not learned to think about other people's feelings and if they do have to wait long, for something like food, they may even become ill.

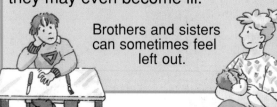

Brothers and sisters can sometimes feel left out.

Playing with a baby

A new baby will not be able to play with you for some time but she may soon start to enjoy watching you play nearby. Once you start to play with her, try to move and speak gently so you don't startle her. Give her plenty of time to react to things and remember that babies cannot concentrate for long. Never do anything she is not happy about.

Babies can only see clearly about 25cm (10in) from their nose.

Babies learn about things by putting them in their mouth, so always ask a grown-up if they are safe.

For the first few weeks, a baby probably has enough to do just getting used to her new surroundings. But she will soon start needing lots of things to look at and listen to.

When babies first learn to hold things, they like being given lots of different things to examine. However, they drop them very easily and don't know how to pick them up again.

Once the baby can sit up, she will be able to play with toys more easily.

Once he can crawl, you can give him things that roll.

93

Babies in nature

Other babies are made, like people, by a mother and a father. In nature, when parents come together so that their sex cells can meet, it is called mating. The moment when the cells join together is called fertilization.

Animals

Animals have their babies in a very similar way to people. During mating, sperm swim towards eggs inside the mother's body. If sperm fertilize the eggs, babies grow in the mother's womb. They are born through her vagina and feed on her milk.

Most animals have more than one baby at a time.

Puppies stay in their mother's womb for nine weeks.

Birds

Baby birds grow outside their mother's body instead of inside. After mating, the mother bird lays her fertilized eggs. Babies grow in the eggs so long as the parents keep them warm by sitting on them.

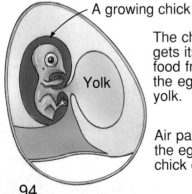

A growing chick

Yolk

The chick gets its food from the egg yolk.

Air passes through the egg shell so the chick can breathe.

When the chick is ready to be born, it cracks open the egg shell with its beak and hatches out.

Eggs that we eat are unfertilized eggs. Chicks could not have grown in them.

94

Insects

Insects lay eggs after mating and fertilization. Most baby insects do not look much like their parents at first. They go through a big change before they are fully grown.

A caterpillar hatches from a butterfly's egg.

The caterpillar changes into a pupa.

The pupa becomes a butterfly.

Fish

Mother fish lay their eggs before they have been fertilized. The father then comes along and puts his sperm on them, and babies start to grow.

Baby fish in their eggs.

Two fish have hatched.

Eye

Caring for the babies

Animals and birds look after their babies until they can manage on their own. Baby insects and fish have to fend for themselves from the start.

Many animals carry their babies out of danger by picking them up in their mouths or giving them a piggy back ride.

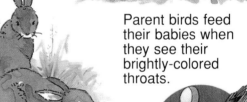

Parent birds feed their babies when they see their brightly-colored throats.

Babies snuggle up to their parents to keep warm.

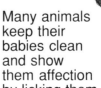

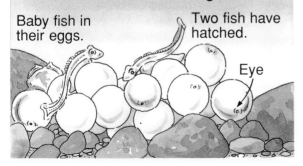

Many animals keep their babies clean and show them affection by licking them.

Index